Sept 2017

RC

A Lottie Lipton ADVENTURE

The Curse of the Cairo Cat

Dan Metcalf

ILLUSTRATED BY
Rachelle Panagarry

MINNEAPOLIS

To Beth, for always believing

This Americanization of *The Curse of the Cairo Cat: A Lottie Lipton Adventure* is published by Darby Creek by arrangement with Bloomsbury Publishing Plc.

Darby Creek
A division of Lerner Publishing Group, Inc.
241 First Avenue North
Minneapolis, MN 55401 USA

For reading levels and more information, look up this title at www.lernerbooks.com.

Main body text set in Stempel Schneidler Std Roman 12/24.
Typeface provided by Adobe Systems.

Library of Congress Cataloging-in-Publication Data

The Cataloging-in-Publication Data for *The Curse of the Cairo Cat: A Lottie Lipton Adventure* is on file at the Library of Congress.
ISBN 978-1-5124-8179-2 (lib. bdg.)
ISBN 978-1-5124-8186-0 (pbk.)
ISBN 978-1-5124-8192-1 (EB pdf)

Manufactured in the United States of America
1-43158-32920-1/12/2017

Contents

Chapter One 1

Chapter Two 19

Chapter Three 33

Chapter Four 46

Chapter Five 62

Glossary 70

Did You Know? 72

Code Breaker 74

A-Maze-ing! 75

Chapter One
London, 1928

Lottie burst through the heavy oak doors and into the darkened corridor.

"Hide . . . Got to hide!" she whispered, her eyes darting about for a suitable place to conceal herself. Along each side of the darkened corridor were glass cabinets and display cases, filled with ancient trinkets and artifacts.

1

"Lottie . . ."

She heard him behind her, not far away now. She could hear each pounding step he took. Her heart raced.

"Got to be quick!" she muttered and darted under a nearby table. Its legs were covered with a red velvet curtain, which she neatly rearranged so it looked like no one had been there.

"I know you're in here . . ." sang the man's voice. He was closer than she had realized. She parted the velvet curtain ever so slightly and peeked out. There he was, silhouetted in the light from the previous room, his large body casting a vast shadow. He stepped forward, closer and closer to her hiding place.

He was next to her now. Her heart beat loudly as she curled herself into a ball, desperate not to be found. She closed her eyes tightly and waited for the moment to come . . .

Suddenly, the entire corridor was flooded with light.

"Professor West?" called a familiar voice. *"Package just arrived for you!"*

"Ooh goody-goody!" said the figure next to Lottie. "Lottie, you can come out now."

Lottie sighed with disappointment. She had been enjoying playing hide-and-seek. She crawled out from her hiding place and smiled up at the seeker, a rotund gentleman with white hair, dressed in a shabby linen suit.

"I win!" she declared. "Honestly Uncle Bert, I was right next to you."

"Not fair," sulked Uncle Bert. "You were supposed to stick to the Egyptian section. This case is clearly from Northern Sudan."

They bickered as they paced along the corridors of the British Museum. Lottie Lipton had lived on the grounds of the museum since she was four, when her archaeologist parents were killed on a dig in Egypt. Since then, she had been cared for by her great uncle, Professor Bertram West. He worked as the  Curator of Egyptology at the British Museum in London, where the two of them lived in a small ramshackle apartment.

In truth, it was Lottie who looked after her uncle; he was famously absent-minded and Lottie would often have to remind him of his appointments, cook his breakfast, and even tie his bow tie for him.

In her spare time, she had the run of the museum. She did not go to school, but instead read voraciously from the museum library and was tutored by her Uncle Bert and her friend Reg, the kindly old caretaker. He too lived on the grounds and was a mine of information; it was from him that Lottie knew how to tune a piano, address a Bishop, and even throw a knife.

It was Reg who had interrupted their game of hide-and-seek and he led them to the main entrance where a package was waiting. Uncle Bert set about opening the packing crate with a crowbar. When he had finished, a large golden statue stood before them. Lottie had never seen anything so beautiful.

"The Golden Cat of Cairo. It's the centerpiece to my new exhibition. The pharaohs worshipped felines, you see, and this was made to commemorate the passing of one of the royal pets."

"It's marvelous," breathed Lottie, unable to take her eyes off it.

"Legend has it that the statue is cursed," continued Uncle Bert. "It comes to life every night and prowls around, causing mischief . . ."

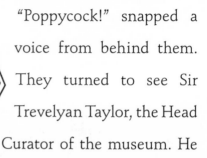

"Poppycock!" snapped a voice from behind them. They turned to see Sir Trevelyan Taylor, the Head Curator of the museum. He was a thin, weasel-faced man and he had never liked Lottie or Uncle Bert. He tried at every opportunity to get them out of their home at the British Museum, not caring for even a second where they might go. He looked the statue up and down, frowning. "Bertram, when will you learn that archaeology is about facts, not spooky curses? Now make sure this beastly object is in position for the grand opening tomorrow. We've got some very important guests coming, and I'm relying on their donations to keep the museum running. If we don't make our target, I'll know who to blame," he said, stalking off.

The Professor looked at his companions and blushed. "Poppycock, of course. There's no such thing as curses." He patted the giant cat on the head. "Ho-hum. We'd better get this in place. The exhibition opens tomorrow."

The night of the grand opening of the exhibition came and Lottie was busy helping her great uncle to prepare. He had to give a

speech in front of a room full of guests and was extremely nervous. Sir Trevelyan's threats hadn't helped.

"You'll be fine," Lottie assured him, practically pushing him onto the podium. The Golden Cat of Cairo stood next to him inside a display case, hidden by a large sheet.

He mumbled through his speech with his eyes glued to his feet until it was time to unveil the main exhibit.

"It . . . ah . . . gives me great pleasure to introduce to you . . ."

Lottie smiled as she prepared to pull away the sheet.

"The splendid . . ."

Uncle Bert was shaking with fear, praying everyone liked his new exhibit.

"The striking . . ."

Here we go! thought Lottie.

"The Golden Cat of Cairo!"

Lottie whipped away the sheet to reveal . . .

Nothing.

The audience gasped and Uncle Bert turned to the empty display case.

"It was here earlier," he said, confused. Lottie rushed to his side. She smiled at the audience, but caught the eye of Sir Trevelyan. He marched up to them and took Uncle Bert aside.

"Honestly Bertram, half of London is here tonight! If you make a fool of the museum again, I won't be responsible for my actions! You have one hour to find that cat, or you'll be asked to leave the museum," he ranted. *"For good!"*

Lottie's smile faded as he marched away.

"Oh, Uncle Bert! We have to find the statue or we'll be homeless! Where did you put it?"

"Here, I promise you!" said Uncle Bert, mopping his brow. "Wait . . . it could be . . ."

"The curse? I thought you said that was poppycock?"

"Trouble brewing?" said Reg, appearing by their side. "'Ere, I found this behind the cabinet."

He handed Lottie a small papyrus scroll, no bigger than the palm of her hand. Inside, it read:

BY NIGHT I PROWL PAST STONE AND SAND, THROUGH OCEANS DEEP TO ANCIENT LANDS. FIND ME WHERE THE RISING SUN SHINES ROUND AND RED—WE'LL HAVE SUCH FUN!

"But what does it mean?" said Lottie.

"It means the curse is real. Very real indeed," muttered Uncle Bert. "As for the riddle, I haven't the faintest idea."

Can you solve the Cairo Cat's riddle? Turn the page to see if you're right!

Lottie, Uncle Bert, and Reg huddled around the tiny scroll, attempting to make sense of the cryptic riddle. Uncle Bert scratched his head and fiddled with his bow tie nervously.

"Oh, it's no good. I'm too nervous to think!"

Lottie rolled her eyes in exasperation and concentrated.

"I'm sure it's quite simple. We just need to take it one step at a time."

"By night I prowl past stone and sand . . ."

"Stone and sand. It must mean the pyramids and the desert," said Lottie.

"Of course! It means it's left the Egyptology section," smiled Uncle Bert.

"Through oceans deep to ancient lands . . ."

"Oh no! It's gone abroad." Uncle Bert's smile fell.

"Or more likely, it's left the African section altogether," said Reg.

"Find me where the rising sun shines round and red—we'll have such fun!"

"The little troublemaker is playing with us!" said Reg.

Lottie tried to concentrate. She knew the words meant something . . . but what? Inspiration hit her in a flash.

"It's talking about Japan. The Land of the *Rising Sun*! The national flag is a red

circle on a white background!"

The three rejoiced, congratulating each other on completing the riddle.

"So what are we waiting for?" said Lottie. "Let's go to ancient Japan!"

Chapter Two

Lottie raced her way through the labyrinth of corridors. Having grown up in the museum, she knew each room like the back of her hand, but the sheer size of the place meant that just getting from one side to another took time, and time was something they didn't have the luxury of tonight.

"Lottie! Slow down!" called her great uncle

Bert, out of breath. He was some way behind her, his size slowing him down. Beside him strode Reg, putting on a good pace for his advanced years. Lottie pressed on, anxious to get to the other side of the museum.

Just as she turned the corner into the Department of Ancient Japanese Antiquities, she noticed too late the familiar shiny wood that meant Reg had been lovingly polishing the floor. She applied her brakes, but continued sliding anyway, through the open doors and straight into the Japanese exhibits. She only came to a halt when she ran into a jade green statue of a dragon and fell backward with a loud thud to the floor. She paused to catch her breath but let out a scream when she saw the ancient statue rock slightly on its base and then come toppling toward her. It seemed to fall in slow motion. She shut her eyes tightly as the dragon pinned her to the floor, each fang of its fearsome smile landing close to her head.

She opened her eyes to find herself unhurt, but nose-to-nose with the monster. Uncle Bert appeared above her and let out a sigh.

"Can I suggest a case of more haste, less speed?"

Lottie reluctantly agreed, but was well aware that they had only an hour to find the cat. She would be having fun, were it not for the threat of being homeless hanging over them. Squirming out from underneath the statue, she brushed herself down.

"Silly thing," she sulked. "What's it doing here anyway?"

"It was a roof charm on one of the imperial palaces," said Uncle Bert, as he and Reg struggled to lift the statue. "The Japanese believed it

would protect them and
ward off evil spirits."

"But *I'm* not evil!" Lottie
complained.

"No, but it must know a mischievous soul
when it sees one!" laughed Reg, polishing the
dragon's nose with a rag.

Recovering from her close encounter with
the dragon, Lottie started to creep among the
exhibits, searching for the large golden figure
of the Cairo Cat. The moon cast a menacing
glow on the room, and a more inventive
imagination may have been scared by some
of the statues, but Lottie had seen the room in
daylight enough times to know better.

She stopped by a large bronze statue of a turtle, its fearsome roaring head and sharp claws glinting in the moonlight. Lottie knew the statue was a symbol of peace and was rather fond of it. She had even nicknamed it Charlie.

"Evening, Charlie," she whispered. "Seen any cats on your travels?"

Ridiculous, she thought. Talking to a lump of metal when her home was at risk. She was about to turn away when she thought she saw something. Her eyes darted back to the turtle and she blinked in disbelief. She looked again, and sure enough, Charlie was facing a different way. His head normally pointed

upward to the right, but now it seemed to be pointing left.

"This way?" she asked, feeling a little foolish. The turtle remained immobile, but its roaring head now wore a cheerful grin.

"Thanks, Charlie," said Lottie, still feeling confused as she walked off to the left. She found herself in front of a display of Samurai armor.

"From the Tokugawa period, I'd say. Around the 1600s."

Lottie turned with a start. Reg grinned behind her.

"How do you know?"

"Y'don't work in this place

for as long as I have without picking up a few facts. The Samurai were warriors who fought in the civil wars, but by the time this suit was in action, they were more like officials, serving their lord. Besides, it says so on the label." He nodded to the explanatory plaque next to the suit and winked at Lottie. Uncle Bert wandered up to them.

"No luck?" he asked. "Hullo? This fellow's got a funny smile."

Uncle Bert had a knack for noticing the smallest of details on an exhibit. Sure enough, the mouthpiece of the helmet had something stuffed into it.

"Another scroll!" exclaimed Lottie.

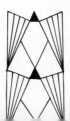

Uncle Bert retrieved the small papyrus scroll from the suit of armor and unfurled it. Lottie took it straight from him, eager to see what the cat had left them this time. She read it out loud:

YOU'VE A LONG WAY TO GO,
BUT YOU'LL DO IT, MY FRIEND.
YOU'LL SEARCH HIGH AND LOW
TO WHERE THE ARMIES END.

"Another riddle!" said Reg. "Me old brain ain't used to all this work."

"Come, come now, old chap," said Uncle Bert. "We can't be disheartened. After all, it's not even a real cat, just a statue."

"Hmm," said Lottie. "It does seem to be giving us the runaround though. The clues are getting harder."

Uncle Bert took the scroll back and adjusted his glasses.

"Nonsense. I refuse to be outwitted by a giant lump of gold." He read through the clue again and sighed deeply.

"Go on then, clever clogs," said Reg. "What does it mean?"

Uncle Bert sat down on a nearby bench with a confused frown.

"I haven't a clue."

Lottie, Reg, and Uncle Bert need your help! Can you solve the clue? Turn the page to see if you're right...

Ten minutes later, the three of them sat on the bench, their heads in their hands. None of them knew how to solve the riddle.

"The trouble is, it could mean any sort of army. But which one? Viking? Roman? Greek?" wondered Uncle Bert.

"It's all Greek to me," laughed Reg, nudging Uncle Bert as he chuckled.

"Really Reg, how can you joke at a time like this?" Uncle Bert said irritably. But Lottie jumped to her feet, an idea striking her.

"That's it!" she said. "Reg, I think this is the one time your awful jokes might actually help us."

"Eh?"

"What do you find at the end of the armies?"

"The handies! Get it?" smiled Reg, waving his hands in front of him.

Now it was Uncle Bert's turn to leap to his feet.

"Of course. Not the 'handies,' but the

Andes!" he shouted, his voice echoing around him. "It's a mountain range in Peru, where an ancient tribe called the Incas used to live."

Lottie smiled and rolled up her sleeves.

"Come on! We've got a statue to catch!"

Chapter Three

The lights blinked on in the Inca room, casting a warm orange glow over the exhibits.

"Here kitty kitty," called Reg with a grin. Lottie laughed and the two of them broke into a fit of giggles. Uncle Bert glared at them, and they struggled to regain control.

"I don't need to remind you how serious this is. We don't have time to be messing around."

"Oh, cheer up, Professor," said Reg. "It's times like these you can see how ridiculous things are."

"Ridiculous?" said Uncle Bert, nearly knocking over a display of beautifully decorated—and very breakable—beakers from the sixteenth century.

"We're chasing around the museum at night, trying to find a giant golden statue shaped like a cat that has mysteriously come alive and escaped. If that ain't ridiculous, I don't know what is!"

They split up, searching the room. Lottie had always loved the Inca room for its color

and energy. The Incas were fascinating and had created the most wonderful beakers with decoratively designed mosaic pictures on them, showing what life must have been like. The pictures were in the brightest turquoise, red, and gold, and when the light hit them, Lottie saw amazing reflections dancing on the walls and ceiling.

"What's so special about the Incas then?" said Reg loudly. Uncle Bert straightened his bow tie and was about to launch into his twenty-minute speech on South American culture, when Lottie jumped in ahead of him.

"They were incredible," she said, suddenly forgetting to be quiet. "They ruled over a huge

area of the Andes, around two thousand miles long, and they had a king that they worshipped like a god. They made roads and temples and bridges and . . ."

She fell silent as she saw a glint of gold in the corner of the room. The cat, at last! She snuck closer, careful not to frighten it away. She could definitely make out two golden ears on the other side of the glass cabinet display. She tiptoed over to the wall and unhooked an old rug that hung there. Creeping closer, Lottie raised the rug, turned the corner, and flung it over the statue's head, diving and grabbing it by the neck so it wouldn't run off.

"Got it, got it, got it!" she yelled. Reg and Uncle Bert came running.

"Well done, Lottie!" said Uncle Bert. "You caught it, single-handed!"

She sat on top of the statue, her arms around the rug that was wrapped around the statue's head. "It doesn't seem to be struggling. Let's take a look at it."

Lottie pulled back the rug to see a gold statue, but it wasn't what she was expecting.

"That ain't a cat!" said Reg.

"No," said Uncle Bert. "It's a llama. They live in Peru, where the Incas would farm them. It's also five hundred years old and priceless."

Lottie looked at the creature. It was large, with pointy ears and a long neck. It could easily have been mistaken for a cat.

"Oops. I suppose I should take this rug off you then," she said to it, sulking a little.

"Actually, it's a tapestry," said Uncle Bert. "It's also five hundred years old and priceless."

Lottie smiled sheepishly at Uncle Bert and hung the tapestry back on the wall, taking great care.

"Ugly thing, ain't it?" said Reg, pointing at the llama. He turned his back on it and watched Lottie hang the tapestry. "If the cat's not here, where's it got to then? That's what I want to—*wah!*"

Reg suddenly fell forward, crashing into the display of beakers. He dropped to the floor and quickly turned to see a few of the delicate objects teetering at the edge of their tables. He dived to catch them as they toppled downward, saving them all like a champion goalkeeper. He clutched them close to his body.

"Are these—?"

"Priceless?" asked Uncle Bert. "Yes! Please, do be more careful."

"I couldn't help it! I was kicked up the bum by—" Reg looked around. "Well, I never. There's no one there."

Lottie turned and looked

at the statue of the llama, which seemed to wear a cheeky smile that it hadn't had before.

"I think I can guess who did it." She walked up to the statue and playfully rubbed its nose. "You should be more careful who you call ugly, Reg." She smiled at the llama, then noticed something tucked behind its ear. "Jackpot!"

She picked out the tiny papyrus scroll and unrolled it. On it was a clue, just like the last one, but as she looked at it Lottie couldn't help but think that this clue might take a little longer to solve. It read:

ZHOO GRQH!
FDQ BRX JXHVV
ZKHUH L'P "URPDQ"
WR QHAW?

"It's complete gibberish," sighed Reg.

"No, it's a code," said Lottie.

Uncle Bert surveyed the scroll briefly and glanced nervously at his pocket watch.

"And we have just under half an hour to crack it," he said, mopping his brow with a handkerchief. "Anyone got any ideas?"

Time is running out for Lottie. Can you help her by cracking the code? Read on to find out if you're right!

Uncle Bert had insisted that they retire to his apartment for a moment, where they could concentrate on the task at hand. The three sat quietly in the untidy room, Uncle Bert at his desk, Lottie on the floor, and Reg on the leather Chesterfield sofa, each with a piece of paper and a pencil, deep in thought. They only had thirty minutes to go, but Uncle Bert assured them that a rest would help them think. He sucked on a dried date as enlightenment hit him.

"Aha!" he barked loudly, making them all jump. "Of course. So simple, yet so effective." He grabbed the scroll from the desk and scribbled furiously on it. Reg and Lottie exchanged looks.

"In ancient Rome, the emperor Julius Caesar used a code called a Caesar Shift to encode important messages. To solve it, you take each letter and replace it with the letter that is three letters before it in the alphabet.

"You mean D becomes A?" said Lottie.

"And E becomes B?" said Reg, catching on.

"Precisely," said Bert, handing them the scroll. "And our message becomes . . ."

WELL DONE!
CAN YOU GUESS
WHERE I'M "ROMAN"
TO NEXT?

Lottie smiled and looked up at Reg and her uncle.

"Gentlemen," she said. "Let's go to ancient Rome.

Chapter Four

The three shadowy figures clung close to each other in the dark of the Department of Ancient Roman Antiques.

"Ow! That's my foot," whispered Lottie.

"Shh!" hissed Uncle Bert.

"What was that?" asked Reg.

"It came from over there."

"It's moving!"

Sure enough, Lottie could make out a shape in the darkness. It was moving slowly and slyly, creeping toward them. She turned to Reg and Uncle Bert.

"You two pounce on it and I'll get the light."

"Right you are, Miss Lottie!"

"On the count of three," whispered Uncle Bert, nervously. "One . . . two . . . *three!*"

The dark figures of Uncle Bert and Reg flew at the creeping shadow ahead of them. Lottie ran to the wall and hit the light switch.

"What on earth are you playing at?" roared the mystery being in front of them. Lottie, blinking in the light, finally saw what they had been tracking. Sir Trevelyan Taylor, Head Curator of the Museum, stood upright with a look of anger and confusion on his face. On seeing their catch, Uncle Bert and Reg let go quickly. Sir Trevelyan glared at Uncle Bert.

"I am disappointed in you, Professor West. Once you were the greatest mind in Egyptology. Now it seems not only are you capable of losing a giant golden statue of an Egyptian cat, but also of attacking your superior!"

"Please, Sir Trevelyan, we were hunting the statue," said Lottie. As the curator's furious gaze turned on her, she regretted opening her mouth.

"Really?" he said in a babyish, patronizing voice. "Well, I hope your great uncle finds it or he will be hunting not just for a cat, but for a job and place to live too!"

"The statue will be ready," said Uncle Bert, barely disguising his anger.

"I hope for your sake it will be," said Sir Trevelyan. "My deadline still stands. You have less than twenty minutes."

The curator marched out

of the Roman section. Uncle Bert, Reg, and Lottie each pulled a face behind his back. They caught each other's eyes and burst out laughing. Uncle Bert and Reg couldn't stop, and Lottie was the first to recover.

"Quiet, you two! We have work to do. Let's split up."

They each went their separate ways and Lottie found herself walking past a large row of display cases. Inside were relics from Roman times—pots, urns, glassware, even old toys. Lottie stared at a carved wooden horse. It reminded her of a toy she once had as a little girl, when she lived in Egypt with her parents. She had loved living there and had vowed to return to Egypt one day and to help finish her parents' work. She looked down sadly but was distracted when she saw what she was standing on.

Under her feet was a perfect recreation of a Roman mosaic, which had been transferred piece by piece from the floor of a villa in North Africa. It showed a slave in a toga, serving a tray of food at a banquet. Lottie had seen it many times before and had marveled at the handiwork. However, she had never noticed that the slave was smiling . . . and pointing. Its fingers pointed to the other side of the large room, past the rest of the exhibits.

"Thank you!" she said aloud to the mosaic and ran off down the gallery. As she passed more display cases, she glanced into them. She couldn't believe her eyes. It seemed as though the whole museum had come alive to help Lottie; a display of Roman knives pointed their blades toward the south of the gallery, a hoard of Roman coins were laid out in a clear arrow and even the model of

a Roman centurion pointed his spear southward.

"Thank you! Thank you!" yelled Lottie to the exhibits around her, no longer feeling foolish at talking to the ancient objects.

She arrived at the south wall of the gallery, Reg and Uncle Bert appearing behind her. They stood before a raised statue of the Roman Emperor Nero. He was delicately sculpted in silver and copper and raised high on a tall marble platform. His left arm was missing, but his right arm pointed skyward.

"There!" shouted Reg suddenly, nodding at the emperor's pointed finger. Around it was wrapped the now familiar scroll from the Cairo Cat.

Reg lifted Lottie to the top of the platform, and she climbed up the statue, finally finding herself on top of Nero's shoulders.

EMPEROR NERO

She reached out to knock the scroll from his fingers. As she scrambled to get down, she could have sworn she heard a voice whisper:

"Well done."

She looked around, but all she could see was Nero, wearing a small smile.

Reg and Uncle Bert peered over the scroll, scratching their heads.

"Let me see!" said Lottie as she rejoined them. They handed it over. It read:

,N3 SW1RD THG3N S1
D12H 4T 2M3T S'T3
,N31G1 2M4H KC1B
.D2B 4T KC1B

"Lottie, we have just ten minutes. If you know how to crack that code," said Uncle Bert, "please, tell us now!"

Use your code breaking skills to decipher the Cairo Cat's clue.
Turn the page to find out if you're right!

Lottie concentrated, focusing only on the clue. It was just letters and numbers, she thought. They might as well face it. All was lost.

And yet . . .

Why were there commas at the beginning of the lines? She knew that a comma always went at the end of a line, like in—

"It's a poem! But backward."

She read it backward, but the numbers still didn't make sense. Reg snatched the scroll from her.

"She's right. And the numbers take the place of the vowels: A, E, I, O, and U."

"So 1 is A, and 2 is E?" said Uncle Bert,

taking the scroll. He slowly read out the
solution.

"As night draws in,
It's time to head
Back home again,
Back to bed."

"Back to bed?" said Lottie. Then it
dawned on her. She dashed to the main
exhibition, where a crowd still waited. Uncle
Bert and Reg jogged breathlessly behind
her, but she couldn't wait. Somewhere, a
grandfather clock hit the first chime of the
hour; time was running out.

She slid into the hall and ran
up onto the podium next to the

covered case where the Cairo Cat was supposed to have been revealed an hour ago.

"Ah, some action finally?" sneered Sir Trevelyan from the back of the room. The crowd laughed.

Lottie, fixing him with a challenging stare, took a deep breath and addressed the crowd.

"Ladies and Gentlemen, I present to you the magnificent, the mischievous, the magical—Golden Cat of Cairo!"

She whipped away the cover on the case, but dared not look. The crowd gasped . . . and broke into applause. Lottie turned to see the golden statue next to her and sighed with relief. She smiled at the crowd, where Sir Trevelyan frowned with anger. The doors burst open to the side of her and Reg and Uncle Bert entered, out of breath, but smiling.

Chapter Five

Uncle Bert and Reg sat at the side of the main hall, looking ready to drop with exhaustion. The exhibition's launch party was over and now most of the guests were leaving, putting on their coats, and strolling off into the night, the cold London air blowing through the hall as they left. Lottie was politely talking to some of the guests and telling them all about their night's adventure. She wasn't sure that they all believed her, but it didn't matter as they all smiled and made nice donations to the museum. She curtsied to a very rich couple as they left and rejoined Reg and Uncle Bert, who were nearly falling asleep.

"That went well," she said. Uncle Bert looked up at her in disbelief.

"Well? *Well?* In what way did it go well?"

"We got the Cairo Cat back in time and everyone enjoyed the party. Sounds like a successful night to me!"

"That darn Cairo Cat!" said Reg, "I've half

a mind to put padlocks on that display case to keep it in. Maybe even iron bars!"

Lottie laughed. "I don't think that will be necessary!"

She stopped laughing as she saw Sir Trevelyan Taylor walking over to them. He looked cross.

"Evening, Sir Trev!" said Reg cheerily. The curator ignored him.

"I don't know how you pulled it off, Bertram, but well done. Everyone is talking about the Golden Cat of Cairo."

"Does that mean we can stay in the museum?" asked Lottie. Sir Trevelyan glared

at her and reluctantly nodded.
They cheered, and Lottie gave
Sir Trevelyan a big hug, which
he didn't seem to enjoy.

"But mark my words,"
he said through gritted teeth as he peeled
Lottie's arms from around him. "I'll find a
way to get rid of you. A museum is not a home
for a dozy professor and his know-it-all niece.
If it's the last thing I do, I'll—"

"How's the donations box looking?"
interrupted Uncle Bert.

"Full," said Sir Trevelyan.

"All because of my know-it-all niece and
this little kitty," said Uncle Bert, patting the

Cairo Cat's display case. "Perhaps you should be grateful, hmm?"

With a final glare, Sir Trevelyan turned and walked away, grumbling.

"We haven't heard the last of him," said Reg.

"Oh well," said Uncle Bert. "I'm sure we'll come up with something if he tries his old tricks again."

Lottie relaxed. Her home was safe once more and she had another adventure to write about in her diary. She glanced over to the Cairo Cat, now proudly standing in its display case. She saw another small scroll, half buried in the sand at the statue's feet.

Peering through the glass, Lottie could just
make out the message:

WHAT FUN!
WHAT DELIGHT!
LET'S PLAY AGAIN
TOMORROW NIGHT!

"Reg," she said with a sigh. "We may need
those padlocks after all."

Glossary

Nero: the Emperor of Rome who ruled from 54 to 68 AD.

British Museum: a large museum in the center of London that contains thousands of objects from world history.

curator: someone who manages a section in a museum and oversees the objects there.

Egypt: a country in Northern Africa. In ancient times, it was ruled by the pharaohs, who built the Pyramids and the Sphinx.

Inca: the ancient civilization from Peru in South America. They ruled over the area from the thirteenth century to the sixteenth century.

Japan: a country in Asia with a rising sun on its flag.

Sudan: a country in Northern Africa, to the south of Egypt.

Did You Know?

- The Incas were great inventors. They invented freeze-dried foods and hanging bridges!

- In ancient Japan, Samurai warriors believed their swords contained spirits and so gave each of their swords a name.

- It is believed that the first cookbook was published in ancient Rome. It was called *De Re Coquinara* and gave recipes for dishes such as boiled ostrich!

- Cat goddesses were worshipped in ancient Egypt. When a cat died, the members of the family who owned it had to shave off their eyebrows as a sign of mourning.

73

Code Breaker

Use the Caesar Shift code from Chapter Three to decipher this message from Lottie. Remember, take each letter and replace it with the letter that is three letters before it in the alphabet. Good luck!

WKDQNV IRU UHDGLQJ PB
ODWHVW VWRUB!
ORRN RXW IRU PB QHAW
DGYHQWXUH,
"VHFUHWV RI WKH VWRUQ"

A-Maze-ing!

The Cairo Cat has escaped
again! Help Lottie get to
the center of the maze.

Did you manage to solve my clues? Look out for Lottie in her next adventure!

A LOTTIE LIPTON ADVENTURE
THE SECRETS OF THE STONE

A mysterious clue appears on the Rosetta Stone.
Can Lottie Lipton, nine-year-old investigator extraordinaire,
solve the clue and beat Bloomsbury Bill?